PRESENTS:

Down at Pollywog Bog

Word Study Buddy Short O KEY:

Green O's: All O's that make the short O sound.

Blue O's: All O's that make the long O sound.

Red O's: All O's that make a different sound than short or long O.

Note to Parents and Teachers:

The color coded words can be used in several different ways.

A teacher can introduce and explain the colors before reading the story. Then, during the reading, the teacher can question students as to why each word is a certain color. (For example, "Before the story I told all of you that the green words were all short O words. Why do you think the word shocked has a green O?")

A second way to use the coding is to NOT say anything about the different colored letters and see if a student observes and questions them organically. If not, spark the conversation yourself. Then, see if students can decipher how words with the same color share a common trait. (For example, a student may say, "I noticed that frog and pollywog are both green and both say the short O sound.")

A third way to use the colors would be to make three groups of students. Next, have each group write down all of the words that share the same color. One group writes the green, one writes the blue, and one writes the red. After the story is read, as a group, students attempt to solve why these words were all placed in the same category.

These are just three ways of using the color coded words in the book. With some creativity and thought there are dozens of ways waiting to be discovered using these words. Have fun creating your own ways today!

Now on with the book! Enjoy!

Who is  ?

Word Study Buddy came from the mind of an elementary school teacher who wanted more interesting phonics based poems and stories for his students to use when decoding words based on their sounds. Steven Mahalic, the author and creator of Word Study Buddy, found that when teaching word study and phonics, his students loved going on "letter sound hunts" in their literature. The problem was that the stories available for teachers to model these hunts were high in demand and short in supply. His solution was to spend hours writing his own stories chock-full of the sounds the students were to search for. After years of creating these delightful rhyming stories he decided to publish them for teachers, parents, and students to use and enjoy.

However, writing these stories was only the beginning. Steven decided to color code the poems for use in the classroom and to include printable word hunt pages at the back of each book that students can use in correlation with the book.

Word Study Buddy hopes this collection of phonics based rhyming stories brings joy to all who read them and also bolsters the word study of the English language that is being done in classrooms across the world.

Thank you for your purchase of this Word Study Buddy product and happy hunting!

Word Study Buddy creator: *Steven Mahalic*

Published by:
Word Study Buddy
Box 1094
339 Hicksville Rd.
Bethpage, NY 11714
www.wordstudybuddy.com

ISBN: 978-1-942437-00-0

Library of Congress Cataloging-in-Publication Data
Mahalic, Steven.
Down at Pollywog Bog/Steven Mahalic.

Summary: A boy hikes the woods and finds a bog with pollywogs who were cursed by a witch.

Includes worksheets for short o phonetic search.

Book & cover design: Darlene Swanson • van-garde.com

Design: Joe Sturges

Illustrations: FlatWorld Solutions, Inc.

For Tim Ferriss,

Without your guide map, what
has become reality would have
stayed an unattained aspiration.

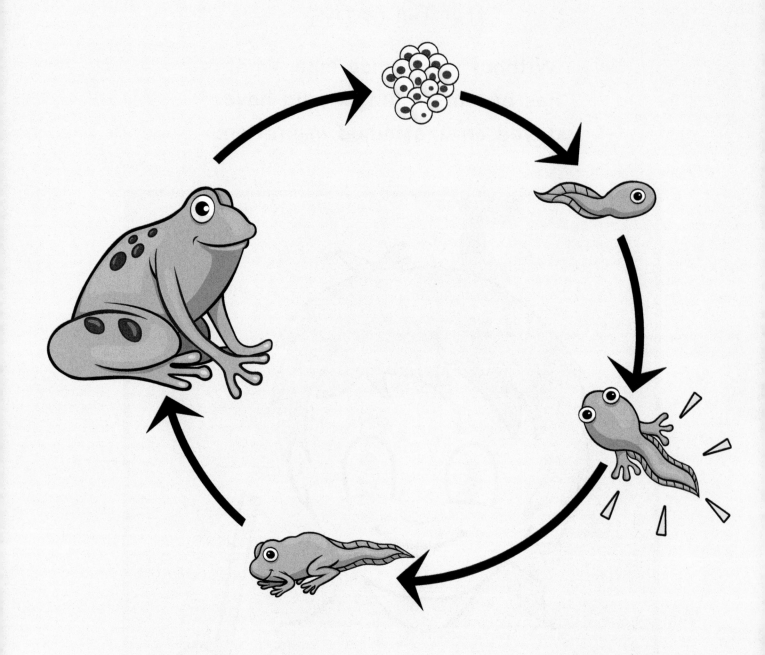

What's another name for tadpole? You know, a baby frog? Well, my friends, believe it or not, it's a pollywog!

Now, what's another name for a swamp?
Where you may find that frog?

Well, my friends, astonishingly, it is called a bog!

On a hike one October day,
I stopped and got a look,
at an odd occurrence I noticed by the brook.

were pollywogs by the lot full!
Dozens, if not more.
They sloshed around that marshy ground.
It was pollywogs galore!

Ordinary tadpoles, these were not.
They talked like you and me!

"How's it going, kid?" one said, with a voice so gravelly.

I asked him his name and age and what he said took me by surprise...

"My name is Bob the pollywog...

Oh, and I'm 45."

"45!" I said, shocked by his response, "I thought pollywogs were young?"

"You see, kid, a witch cursed this place and gave us talking tongues."

I said, "That doesn't sound so bad. Talking is quite nice."

He shot back, "We thought so too, but at a hefty price!"

I found out the witch's deal was to let the pollywogs speak, but they were never allowed to grow older or to leave the creek.

So stuck they stay, in the woods, half-grown up forever.

So if you stumble across Pollywog Bog, remember, that witch is clever!

Don't make a deal that sounds too good to be true because it just might be.

Keep on trotting past Pollywog Bog and live content and witch-free!

Short O Words (the o makes the sound, like in mop)

Long O Words (the o makes the sound, like in open)

_____   _____

_____   _____

_____   _____

_____   _____

_____   _____

_____   _____

_____   _____

_____   _____

_____   _____

_____   _____

_____   _____

_____   _____

_____   _____

Name: _____   **Date:** _____

Other Words

(the word has an o but doesn't make either the long or short o sound, like in word)

_____   _____

_____   _____

_____   _____

_____   _____

_____   _____

_____   _____

_____   _____

_____   _____

_____   _____

_____   _____

_____   _____

_____   _____

_____   _____

_____   _____

Word List

another
for
tadpole
you
know
frog
or
not
pollywog
now
astonishingly
bog
on
one
October
stopped
got
look
odd
occurrence
noticed
brook
oh
good

uncommon
one
no
frogs
a-hopping
those
pollywogs
lot
dozens
more
sloshed
around
ground
pollywogs
galore
ordinary
tadpoles
how's
going
voice
so
took
Bob
shocked

response
thought
young
tongues
doesn't
sound
shot
too
found
out
to
allowed
grow
older
woods
half-grown
forever
across
don't
sounds
trotting
content

Teacher Answer Key

Short o Words (the o makes the sound, like in mop)	Long o Words (the o makes the sound, like in open)	Other (the word has an o but doesn't make either the long or short o sound, like in word)
frog	tadpole	another
not	know	you
pollywog	October	or
astonishingly	noticed	now
bog	oh	occurrence
on	no	for
October	those	one
stopped	tadpoles	look
got	going	brook
odd	so	good
uncommon	grow	uncommon
frogs	older	content
a-hopping	half-grown	one
pollywogs	don't	dozens
lot		more
not		around
sloshed		ground
Bob		galore
shocked		ordinary
response		how's
shot		voice
trotting		took
		thought
		young
		tongues
		doesn't
		sound
		to
		found
		out
		allowed
		woods
		forever
		across
		too

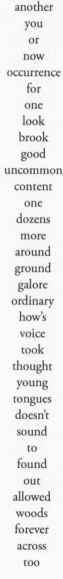

Note to teachers- There is no need for students to find all the words on the word hunt. Use your discretion.

Note to Teachers

When writing these Word Study Buddy stories, I tried adding elements that can be touched upon in other areas of curriculum while still being full of the phonics sound each particular book is themed upon. Above all, I wanted them to be entertaining. In *Down at Pollywog Bog* three areas for inter-disciplinary instruction are science, character education, and English Language Arts.

Science tie-ins: The most obvious tie-in to science is the frog life cycle, but the pond habitat is touched upon, as well. A teacher could easily use this as an entry point or reference point when discussing either science topic.

Character Education tie-ins: This story does have a moral to it, which can be summarized as—be careful who you associate with—which is exemplified by the relationship between the witch and pollywog. A lesson could easily be sparked about the old saying, "if something is too good to be true it probably is." This is a perfect story to discuss the importance of knowing who and what one is getting oneself into in all situations.

English Language Arts tie-ins: In accordance with the moral, this story could be a reference point when learning about fables. Teachers can also use the different terms for tadpole (pollywog) and swamp (bog) as an introductory lesson for teaching synonyms.

No matter how you decide to use this story or any Word Study Buddy stories in the future, I hope the primary benefit you take from it is the whimsical and entertaining nature.

Steven Mahalic

Thank you for your purchase and I hope you enjoyed the book.

Other titles to look for:

Short A: The Happy Black Bat

Short E: Chet the Vet

Short I: Itchy Twitchy Ritchie From Wichita City

Short U: My Uncle's Old Rusty Trunk

Coming soon:

Long Vowels books!

Titles such as:

Unicorns That Wear Cute Blue Boots

Joe the Glowing Goat

CPSIA information can be obtained
at www.ICGtesting.com
Printed in the USA
LVOW05*1221080216

474004LV00005B/4/P

9 781942 437000